THIS TREE COUNTS!

Alison Formento   Illustrated by Sarah Snow

Albert Whitman & Company • Chicago, Illinois

E FOR

To Dan, who counts most of all—A. F.
For Will, Cosmo, and Gil—S. S.

Printed on recycled paper containing 50% post-consumer content.

Library of Congress Cataloging-in-Publication Data

Formento, Alison.
This tree counts! / by Alison Formento ; illustrated by Sarah Snow.
p. cm.
Summary: Before they begin planting new trees, Mr. Tate tells his students to
listen closely as the lone tree behind their school counts out ten ways it serves
the needs of different animals.
ISBN 978-0-8075-7890-2
(1. Trees—Fiction. 2. Schools—Fiction. 3. Counting.) I. Snow, Sarah, III. II. Title.
PZ7.F6764Th 2010
(E)—dc22
2009024283

10 9 8 7 6 5 4 3 2 1 BP 14 13 12 11 10 09

The art is collage created by hand and digitally,
with found papers, acrylics, and watercolors.

The design is by Nick Tiemersma.

For more information about Albert Whitman & Company,
please visit our web site at www.albertwhitman.com.

Only one tree stood behind Oak Lane School.
It needed friends.

So Mr. Tate's class decided to plant more trees.

The children got ready to dig.

Mr. Tate said, "Wait! Our big tree has a story to tell."

The wind began to blow, and
the giant tree shook its leaves.
"Trees can't talk," Jake said.
Mr. Tate said, "Trees will speak
only if you listen closely."

Everyone leaned an ear
against the tree. This is
what they heard...

One owl sits high on my branches,
waiting for the moon.

TWO spiders cling tight to webs, spinning all day long.

Three squirrels skitter across my boughs,
playing hide-and-seek.

Four robins sing from a nest,
calling out hellos.

Five caterpillars inch by, building new cocoons.

"They'll turn into butterflies soon," Shin said.
"Shhh!" said Eli. "The tree wants us to listen."

Six ants march from leaf to leaf, crawling along my bark.

Seven crickets rub strong long legs, chirping at the sun.

Eight flies buzz all around, searching for some food.

Nine ladybugs climb around my trunk, exploring before they fly.

Ten earthworms glide over my roots,
munching rich moist soil.

I am a home for so many,
all living safe and free!

Everyone looked up at the giant tree.
It waved its leaves.

One fell on Amy's head.

"What did you hear?" Mr. Tate asked.

"This tree counts!" Jake said.

"What else is great about trees?" Mr. Tate asked.

"They make cool shade," said Natalie.

"This tree washes the air, too," said Mr. Tate.

"Trees can't wash," Jake said.

"They do wash!" Mr. Tate said. "They take in dirty air and send out fresh oxygen to breathe."

Everyone took a deep breath.

"This tree is so pretty. Can we name it?" Natalie asked.

"Trees don't have names," Jake said.

"They do have names!" said Mr. Tate. "We call this an oak. That's what we're planting today. These oak saplings will grow and make acorns."

"Squirrels love acorns," Jake said. "They gather them in the fall."

"That's right," Mr. Tate said. "And the ones they don't eat, you can plant to grow your own oak trees. Can you think of some other kinds of trees?"

"We have an apple tree in our yard," Shin said.

"Palm trees grow where it's warm," said Eli.

"What about Christmas trees?" Jake asked.
"Those are fir trees," Mr. Tate said.
"They stay green all year long."

"This tree is so big," Natalie said. "I wish I could live up there."
"I have a tree house," Eli said. "I made up a poem about it."

Tree house, tree house, in the sky,
grow some wings and you can fly!
Birds can nest, and so can I.

"I don't have a nest," said Jake. "I live in an apartment.
But we're building a house, and it's all made of wood!"

"My guitar is made from wood, too," Shin said.

"My dad made a wooden picnic table for our yard," said Natalie.

"My pencil is made of wood!" shouted Eli.

Jake put his arms around the tree. He looked up through the branches. "Trees sure can do a lot!"

Mr. Tate nodded. "Now you're ready to dig."

Everyone planted…

one, two, three,
four, five, six,
seven, eight, nine,
ten trees.

Ten baby trees.

"Have fun with your new friends," Shin told the giant tree.
The wind blew, and the tree waved again.

The new trees waved, too!